To Avery, who would most probably
cuddle an alligator, too! - S.S.

To Madeleine, my sweet little hungry alligator - J.D.

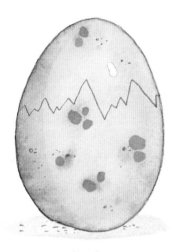

tiger tales
5 River Road, Suite 128, Wilton, CT 06897
Published in the United States 2021
Originally published in Spain 2020
by Little Tiger Press Ltd.
Text copyright © 2020 Steve Smallman
Illustrations copyright © 2020 Joëlle Driedemy
ISBN-13: 978-1-68010-245-1
ISBN-10: 1-68010-245-1
Printed in China
LTP/2800/3493/1020
10 9 8 7 6 5 4 3 2 1

For more insight and activities, visit us at www.tigertalesbooks.com

THE ALLIGATOR WHO CAME FOR DINNER

by STEVE SMALLMAN

Illustrated by JOËLLE DREIDEMY

tiger tales

Little Lamb was a lamb, and Wolf was a wolf.
And they were the very best of friends.
Sometimes they did lamby things,
like skipping through meadows.
And sometimes they did wolfy
things, like howling at the moon.

AROOO

BAAAA

One night, they found an egg. A big egg!

"Ooh, yummy!" cried Wolf. "I can make an omelet!"
Little Lamb gave Wolf a hard stare.
"No, Wolf. Not an omelet. A baby bird."

Little Lamb made Wolf check all the nests nearby, but nobody had lost an egg.

"What do you do with a lost egg?" wondered Wolf.
"It's not 'lost,' Wolf," whispered Little Lamb. "It's found!"
Then she picked up the egg and carefully
carried it home.

"You can live with us!" Little Lamb told the egg. Wolf nodded and was trying not to think of how delicious an omelet would be when . . .

CRACK!

went the egg.

And out popped a little alligator!

Hello, Omelet!

Omelet climbed onto Wolf's shoulder and nibbled his ear.

"He's hungry!" laughed Little Lamb.

"But what do alligators eat?" wondered Wolf.

Ouch!

They soon found out that alligators eat everything. Even wolf tails.

It was getting late, so Wolf tucked Little Lamb into bed and found a blanket for Omelet.

But the alligator had already settled down . . . on Wolf's bed!

"I'm not sure," yawned Wolf, sinking into his chair, "that taking an alligator home was such a good idea!"

Then Omelet scrambled up and snuggled against Wolf's chest.

And Wolf, who had never been cuddled by an Omelet before, thought that maybe everything would be okay.

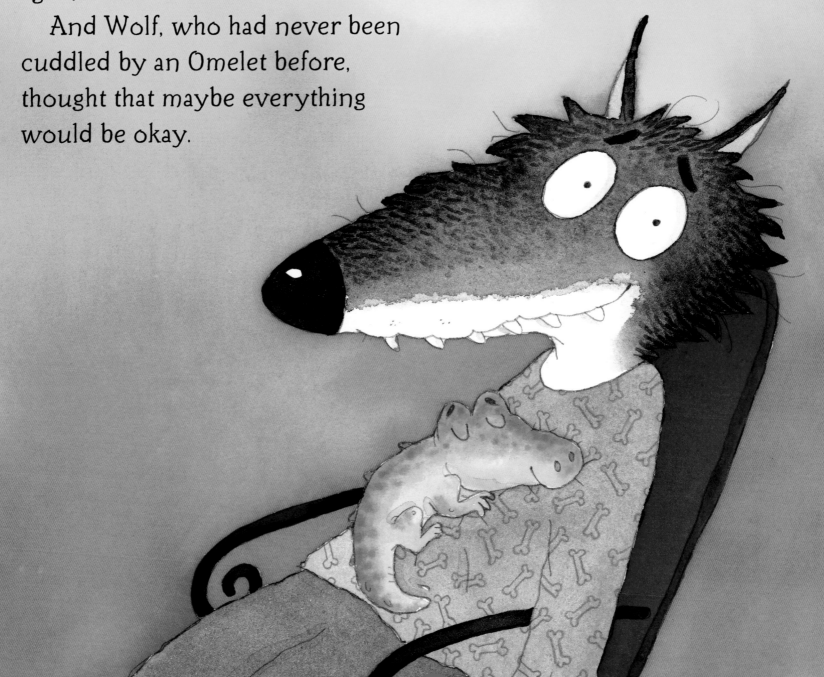

But in the morning ...
"What happened to my kitchen?" cried Wolf.
"Omelet happened!" said Little Lamb.
"We'd better take him out for a walk," sighed
Wolf, "before he makes any more of a mess!"

. . . and gave them all a big, slobbery kiss!

Well, that was a surprise!

What a cute little fella!

I knew he wouldn't hurt us!

Wolf and Little Lamb chased Omelet through the trees . . .

SPLASH!

. . . where Omelet dove in for a swim!

"He'll gobble us up!" cried a bunny.

"Omelet wouldn't hurt a fly!" called Wolf.
"He's only little."

"He is now," grumbled
Badger. "But not for long!"

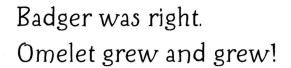

Badger was right.
Omelet grew and grew!

But even though he was noisy,
and messy, and nibbly, Wolf
and Little Lamb loved him.
And Omelet loved
them right back.

Pretty soon, everyone in the forest loved Omelet.
Well, almost everyone.

"You won't be laughing when that alligator gobbles you up!" warned Badger as black rain clouds darkened the forest. That night, there was a terrible storm.

And in the morning, the forest was flooded.
"Omelet is missing!" cried Little Lamb.
They rushed out to look for him.

All the animals searched high and low.

Poor little fella.

Lost in the woods

With all this water.

A set of muddy footprints led them down to the river, which was flowing deep and fast.

Mommy Duck called from the riverbank. "Help! My ducklings! They're being swept away!"

"Who will save them?" wailed the animals.

"Omelet!" cried Little Lamb, pointing at the alligator swimming bravely toward the ducklings.

Then everyone GASPED as Omelet opened his mouth and . . .

SNAP!

... the ducklings disappeared inside!

Eek!

"He gobbled them up!" shrieked the rabbits.

"I told you this would happen!" bellowed Badger.

Omelet trotted up to the animals, who shrank back in fright.

He opened his mouth . . .

DON'T EAT US, TOO!

. . . and out jumped one, two, three little ducklings.

"Great job, Omelet!" cheered Wolf, and Little Lamb gave him a great big hug.

"HOORAY FOR OMELET!" everyone cheered.

"Well, it's like I've always said," blustered Badger.
"It's very useful to have an alligator around!"

Little Lamb gave Badger a hard stare, and Badger stopped
talking. Then Wolf took Little Lamb and Omelet home,
where they all lived snappily ever after.